Feel the Summer

Feel the Summer

by Sarah L. Thomson • illustrated by Kana Yamada

MILK &
COOKIES
PRESS ™

Distributed by Publishers Group West

In the summer, morning glories
reach over the fence
to say hello.

We're going to our friend's house.
He doesn't have a pool.
But if he gets one
we'll be ready.

An afternoon at the park
stretches out like warm taffy.
Nothing moves.
Nothing breathes.
The stone elephant and
I wait for a breeze
to bring us back to life.

It's so hot
the butterflies
have melted.

I wish I could spend all day
leaning into the freezer's icy kiss.
Maybe I'll find a polar bear cub
clambering over glaciers of popsicles
and mountains of ice cream bars.

A balloon tugs me
up the stairs
I thought I was
too tired to climb.

The city bakes
like bread in an oven.
When I hold your hand
we walk so slowly
that the sunlight opens up
to let us in.

In the cool of the car
mom and dad
watch us safely home
and the summer night
wraps itself
around our shoulders
like velvet.

Our car is packed with
towels, shovels
blankets, juice
peanut butter and jelly
sandwiches
inner tubes
books
hats, sunscreen
one dog
two parents
and my sister and me
glued to the backseat
waiting, waiting, waiting.

It's a long drive.
Four songs too long,
three books too long,
two naps too long,
one temper tantrum too long,
a much too long
drive to the beach.

Let's go! Come on!
Hurry, everybody!
The ocean might be used up
by the time we get there!

Salty breeze promises,
glimpse of blue beckons
whitecaps wave to us—
jump in, jump in!

Bare feet and broiling sand—
it's the hop skip jump ouch
dance to the spot
where the sand is silky wet
between our toes.

Cool water kisses us.
Waves give bear hugs.
The ocean's so happy
to see us again.

To Naya and Rowan
in memory of Alaska summers
—S.L.T.

With love to my parents and friends
—K.Y.

Feel the Summer
Copyright © 2006 ibooks, inc.
Text copyright © Sarah L. Thomson, 2006
Illustrations copyright © Kana Yamada, 2006

A publication of
Milk & Cookies Press, a division of ibooks, inc.

Distributed by Publishers Group West
1700 Fourth Street, Berkeley, CA 94710

This book is a work of fiction.
Any resemblance to actual events or locales or persons,
living or dead, is entirely coincidental.

ibooks, inc.
24 West 25th Street, 11th floor, New York, NY 10010

ISBN: 1-59687-174-1
First ibooks, inc. printing: May 2006
10 9 8 7 6 5 4 3 2 1

Editor - Dinah Dunn
Associate Editor - Robin Bader

Designed by Edie Weinberg

Library of Congress Cataloging-in-Publication Data
available

Manufactured in China